The Princess who had no Fortune

For Leo and Max
U.J.

To Olly, Harri and Bella, with love
S.G.

ORCHARD BOOKS
338 Euston Road, London NW1 3BH
Orchard Books Australia
Level 17/207 Kent Street, Sydney, NSW 2000

First published in 2014 by Orchard Books

ISBN 978 1 40831 276 6

Text © Ursula Jones 2014
Illustrations © Sarah Gibb 2014

The rights of Ursula Jones to be identified as the author and of Sarah Gibb
to be identified as the illustrator of this work have been asserted by them in
accordance with the Copyrights, Designs and Patents Act, 1988.

A CIP catalogue record for this book is available from the British Library.

1 3 5 7 9 10 8 6 4 2

Printed in China

Orchard Books is a division of Hachette Children's Books,
an Hachette UK company.

www.hachette.co.uk

The Princess who had no Fortune

Ursula Jones 👑 Sarah Gibb

ORCHARD

Once there was a princess who lived in a castle on top of a hill with her father and her cat, Geoffrey.

One Thursday morning, the princess woke to the sound of rain – pattering onto her pillow. "Wake up, Geoffrey," she cried, tumbling out of bed. "We've sprung another leak!"

"It never rains but it pours through our roof," thought Geoffrey, as the princess ran about the castle, placing Royal Buckets under all the drips.

It took ages so the princess was late for breakfast. There, waiting for her, was a golden envelope propped against the empty toast rack. Inside was an invitation from the king and queen of The-Kingdom-Next-Door. It said:

Please come to our ball this Saturday night, when the prince, our son, will choose a bride from among the guests.

"What if she doesn't want to be chosen?" the princess asked Geoffrey. "I've no time for princes," she said. "They are only good for declaring things open and sitting on thrones. I do love a good dance, though, so I'll go. If the prince chooses me, I'll just say, 'no thank you' and he can marry the runner-up."

The princess ran to the Royal Wardrobe to
find her ball gown. It was full of
moth holes. "Oh no!" she said. "Now I'll
have to buy a new one."

She went to look in the Royal Purse, but it was empty.
"As usual," thought Geoffrey.
"I'll try Dad," said the princess.

The princess ran down the enormous, overgrown garden. At the very bottom, she found the king's shed. Inside was a whirl of feathers.

"Please, Father," panted the princess, "may I have some money for a new ball gown?"

The king shook his head. "Haven't a penny, my love. Spent it all on feathers."

"No wonder there wasn't any toast," thought Geoffrey.

"Not to worry," chuckled the king. "We'll have bags of money once I've invented my new flying machine!"

But the princess *did* worry. The king had already invented six flying machines, and not one of them had worked.

"At your last crash," warned the princess, "you dented your crown."

"Trust me," said the king, stirring a pot of glue in a regal manner. "Oh! By the way, I've asked all my subjects up to the castle to watch my first test flight on Saturday afternoon. There'll be tea afterwards in the garden." Glue sloshed onto his Royal Robes. "Cupcakes would be nice."

"Forget the ball, Geoffrey," said the princess as they fought their way back through the garden. "We are out of cash. Thank goodness there is some flour left in the Royal Larder for cupcakes."

The princess wrote to the king of The-Kingdom-Next-Door to say she could not come to the ball. Then she pedalled down to the post box on the Royal Bike. Everyone smiled and shouted, "See you on Saturday, Princess." The princess smiled back.

"Listen, Geoffrey," she puffed as she pedalled home, "the entire kingdom is coming to tea, our castle is a mess and the king is gluing feathers. That leaves just you and me to get everything ready in time."

"Some chance," thought Geoffrey.

POST BOX

The princess set to work on the castle. She scrubbed, swept and polished for hours on end. Geoffrey went to sleep.

At midnight, the princess flopped into bed, exhausted. Suddenly she sat bolt upright. "The garden!" she gasped. "It's a jungle!" Quickly she wrote out a notice. Then she woke Geoffrey. "Cats can see in the dark, so run and pin this to the castle gates, please."

"The trouble with me," thought Geoffrey sleepily, "is I'm just too talented." But he did it.

WANTED
URGENTLY:
a gardener

The next morning, the princess prepared one hundred cupcakes.
But just as they were coming out of the Royal Oven, she dropped them all.

"Eugh!" thought Geoffrey, jumping clear. "Not cupcakes! Yuck cakes!" And he went
to sleep. But the doorbell woke him up. "That will be the gardener," thought Geoffrey.

The princess ran to open the castle door. "Hello," she smiled at the young man
on the doorstep. "Can you start straight away?"

"Certainly," he replied, looking rather startled.

"You'd better begin by cutting the lawns," she said. Then she ran back to the
kitchen to make new cupcakes.

The princess burnt that batch. She tried again. The next batch turned out hard as stones. She tried again. These looked a bit wonky, but the princess decided that they would have to do.

"Now for the icing," she said. But the icing melted and stuck to the Royal Kitchen Table. It stuck to the floor. It stuck to Geoffrey. It stuck to the princess.

"Yuck!" she said and ran away from it into the garden, only to find the gardener cutting the lawn with his penknife! He'd done a patch the size of a plate.

The princess called the gardener in for a coffee break.
"You are an even worse gardener than I am a cook,"
she said, as they mopped up icing sugar. "How are we
going to be ready for the visitors tomorrow afternoon?"

"What you need," said the gardener, "is a prince in shining armour."

"No, I don't," said the princess, as they scraped out the mixing bowls
together. "I need clever people who can bake cupcakes.
Princes only know how to eat them. And princes don't
cut lawns, they just stroll on them. Take that
Prince-Next-Door. He sounds much
too big for his Royal Boots."

The gardener thought hard. "Try making a wish to your fairy godmother," he suggested.

The princess was pretty sure that her dad had never fixed her up with one of those, but she made a wish, out of politeness.

The princess looked so downhearted that
the gardener asked shyly if she would care to dance.
"It always cheers me up no end," he said.
"Me too," agreed the princess.

The kitchen floor was too sticky for dancing, so they went to the castle
ballroom. They danced and danced, and Geoffrey went to sleep.
At last, the gardener remembered he should go home.
"We'll try harder tomorrow," the princess told Geoffrey
as she climbed into bed.

Very early the next morning, Geoffrey went into the garden to do a bit of bird-watching.
He'd hardly begun when, to his surprise, the gardener rode up to the castle gates on a
handsome horse. Two carthorses came after him, pulling a cartload of gardeners.
Out they all sprang, and spread across the garden. Within an hour, the garden was perfect.

Geoffrey blinked. What a makeover! Then up drove a second cart. Ten chefs, each
carrying a tray of cupcakes, stepped out and filed through the Royal Kitchen Door.

As the clock on the castle turret struck the hour, they all hurried away,
leaving the gardener to fiddle about uselessly, straightening a hollyhock.

The princess opened her bedroom window and nearly fell out with surprise.
"Geoffrey," she laughed, "Dad *did* get me a fairy godmother. She's answered my wish!"

"That gardener is the most peculiar-looking fairy godmother I've ever seen,"
thought Geoffrey.

That afternoon, the visitors flooded in. Geoffrey went to sleep. The princess poured tea and the gardener served the cupcakes.

When the princess thanked him, he said, "Anything for the girl who is nearly as bad a cook as I am a gardener." And they laughed.

Then a far-off voice called, "Hello, all!"
It was the king, up in the clock tower.

"Hello, Sire," the visitors called up to him.

The king tootled a Royal Fanfare through
a rolled-up newspaper. "Sorry: no Royal
Trumpet. Sold it," he shouted down.

"Here I go." The king waggled his wings.

"Maiden voyage of my flying machine."
And he jumped.

"Flap! Flap your wings!" shrieked the princess in alarm.

"Flap, Sire!" begged his subjects. But although the king flapped like mad, he was definitely falling and falling – to the ground!

The gardener snatched the Royal Tablecloth from the table. Cupcakes scattered far and wide. "Follow me!" he ordered the visitors, and he sprinted to the bottom of the clock tower. Everyone ran after him, and together they all held out the tablecloth.

Down the king fell, and – *plop*! – he landed in the tablecloth, safe and sound. Everyone cheered.

The king clapped the gardener on the back. "Splendid catch, young man! You deserve a rich reward, but I'm a bit low on cash just now."

"Offer him your daughter's hand in marriage, instead," the princess whispered to her father.

"No thanks," replied the gardener.

"Why not?" The king looked extremely huffy. "She's perfect."

"Because I don't love the princess. I love the cook."

That made the princess very sad indeed.

Geoffrey bristled. "Come clean. You're no gardener," he hissed. "He's a fairy godmother," he told everyone.

That set them all arguing.

"Funny sort of fairy godmother."

"No wand."

"No wings."

"I'm *not* a fairy godmother," said the gardener.

He turned to the princess. "I pretended I was, to help you. You had too much to do, Miss Cook."

"Thank you," said the princess. "But I'm not the cook."

"Wait a minute," the king interrupted. "Who is everyone, if they're not who they say they are?"

"I'm the princess," said the princess.

"And I'm the Prince-Next-Door," sighed the gardener.

"Of course he is!" everyone exclaimed. "He's in all the magazines! We didn't recognise him without his crown."

The Prince-Next-Door looked glum. "The princess won't marry me now she knows who I really am. I came to visit her because she was the only princess who refused to come to the ball. I thought she might be my sort of girl. And she is. She's wonderful." He shrugged unhappily. "Then there was a muddle, and now she wants to marry the gardener, who is not me, who wants to marry the cook, who is not her."

"Ahhh," everyone sighed.

"And now I'm late for my own ball. I have to choose a bride. Father insists. Goodbye."

"Sorry to butt in," the princess said. "If you want to marry me, Prince, why don't you ask me?"

"Because you think that princes only stroll on lawns and eat cupcakes. You think I'm too big for my boots."

"But I love you – and your boots!"

"Oh well, then," said the Prince-Next-Door with a broad smile, "let's get married!"

The princess smiled back. "Yes, let's."

So they did. And in all the excitement, no one remembered
that Geoffrey had spoken. Who ever heard of a talking cat?

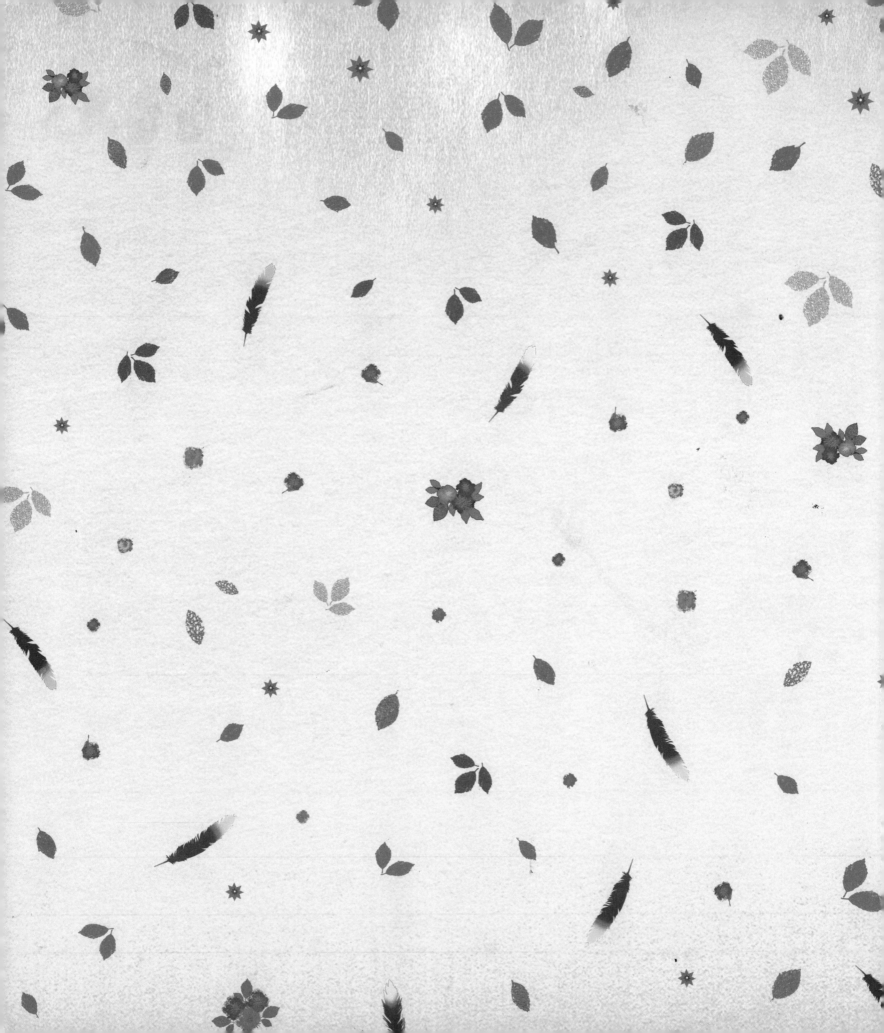